A firefighter needs rest.
It is bedtime at the firehouse.

Edward saves the day.
There is a big parade to celebrate.

Edward climbs the ladder and rescues the kitten. "Good work!" the firefighters cheer.

A kitten is stuck up a tree!
"Who will save her?" asks a firefighter.
Edward volunteers, "Let me!"

They return to the firehouse.
After lunch, the alarm rings again.
This time, it is a real emergency!

But he needs help coming down.
Lifesaving is a firefighter's most important job.

Edward practices going up the ladder.

Everyone works together.

Judy opens the fire hydrant.
The water is so strong it knocks Edward off his feet.

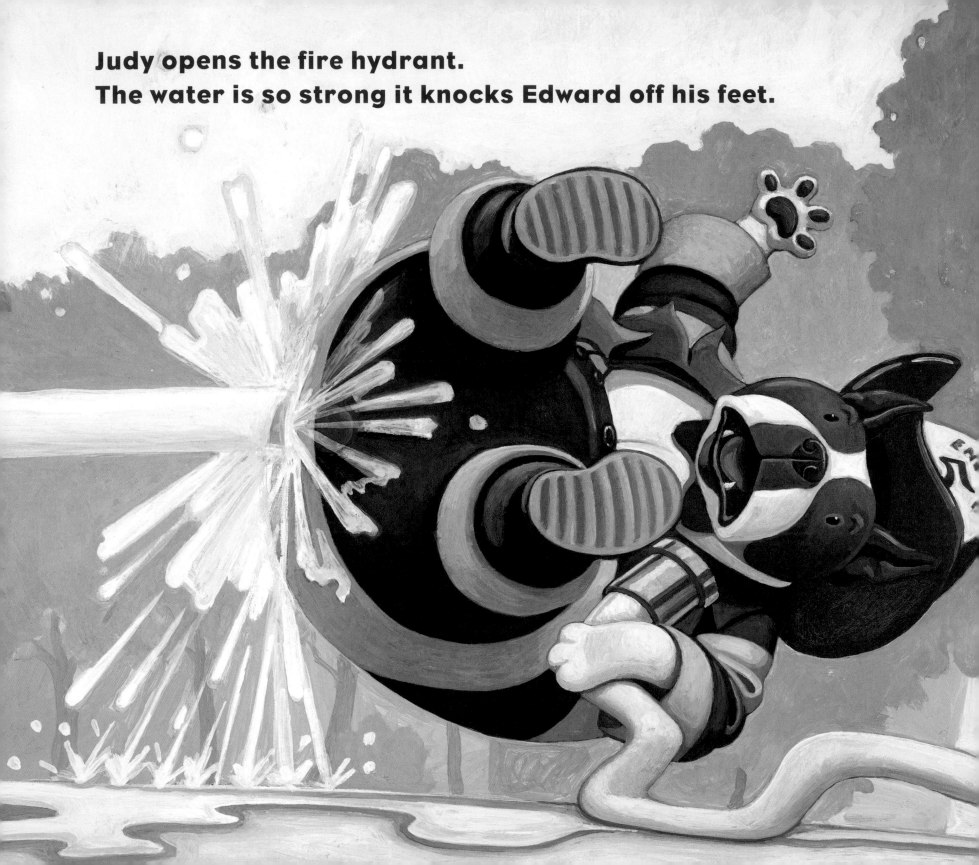

"Hang on, Edward!" a firefighter calls.
The fire engine speeds away.

Everyone hurries down the fire pole.

"This is a fire drill," calls the fire chief.
The firefighters spring into action!

Suddenly, the alarm rings!

"This is where we live,"
says a firefighter.

Edward climbs into the driver's seat.
He steers to the right. He steers to the left.

Everyone helps.
"A clean fire engine is a happy fire engine," says a firefighter.

Mrs. Speckle, the fire chief, shows them around.
"First you can help wash the fire truck," she says.
"Later we will have a practice fire drill."

Edward tries on a shiny red fire hat.

Edward wants to be a firefighter.
One day he and Judy visit a firehouse.

Text and illustrations copyright © 2010 by Mark Teague
All rights reserved. Published by Orchard Books, an imprint of Scholastic Inc., *Publishers
since 1920.* ORCHARD BOOKS and design are registered trademarks of Watts Publishing
Group, Ltd., used under license. SCHOLASTIC and associated logos are trademarks and/or
registered trademarks of Scholastic Inc.

Library of Congress Cataloging-in-Publication Data

Teague, Mark.
Firehouse! / by Mark Teague. — 1st ed. p. cm.
Summary: Edward and his cousin Judy come for a visit to the firehouse and learn how
everything works with some unexpected results.
ISBN 978-0-439-91500-7 (reinforced bdg. for library use)

[1. Fire departments—Fiction. 2. Fire extinction—Fiction.] I. Title.
PZ7.T2193825Fir 2010   [E]—dc22   2009012100

10 9 8 7 6 5 4 3 2   10 11 12 13 14
Printed in Singapore   46
Reinforced Binding for Library Use
First edition, May 2010

The artwork was created using oil paints.
The text was set in 20-point Eagle Book.
Book design by Charles Kreloff

MARK TEAGUE

FIREHOUSE!

ORCHARD BOOKS • NEW YORK

An Imprint of Scholastic Inc.